Best Friends
in the Snow

by Angela Shelf Medearis

Illustrated by Ken Wilson-Max

My First Hello Reader!
With Game Cards

SCHOLASTIC INC.

Cartwheel ·B·O·O·K·S·®

New York   Toronto   London   Auckland   Sydney

It's cold outside,
but we are warm,
with hats and coats
and mittens on.

Hello, Family Members,

Learning to read is one of the most important accomplishments of early childhood. **Hello Reader!** books are designed to help children become skilled readers who like to read. Beginning readers learn to read by remembering frequently used words like "the," "is," and "and"; by using phonics skills to decode new words; and by interpreting picture and text clues. These books provide both the stories children enjoy and the structure they need to read fluently and independently. Here are suggestions for helping your child.

- Have your child think about a word he or she does not recognize right away. Provide hints such as "Let's see if we know the sounds" and "Have we read other words like this one?"
- Encourage your child to use phonics skills to sound out new words.
- Provide the word for your child when more assistance is needed so that he or she does not struggle and the experience of reading with you is a positive one.
- Encourage your child to have fun by reading with a lot of expression . . . like an actor!

I do hope that you and your child enjoy this book.

> —Francie Alexander
> Reading Specialist,
> Scholastic's **Learning Ventures**

Activity Pages
In the back of the book are skill-building activities. These are designed to give children further reading and comprehension practice and to provide added enjoyment. Offer help with directions as needed and encourage your child to have FUN with each activity.

Game Cards
In the middle of the book are eight pairs of game cards. These are designed to help your child become more familiar with words in the book and to play fun games.

- Have your child use the word cards to find matching words in the story. Then have him or her use the picture cards to find matching words in the story.
- Play a matching game. Here's how: Place the cards face up. Have your child match words to pictures. Once the child feels confident matching words to pictures, put cards face down. Have the child lift one card, then lift a second card to see if both match. If the cards match, the child can keep them. If not, place the cards face down once again. Keep going until he or she finds all matches.

To Deborah, Charles,
Danielle, and David Patton,
our friends in any weather
—A.S.M.

To my best friends Taz and Lin
—K.W.M.

Text copyright © 1999 by Angela Shelf Medearis.
Illustrations copyright ©1999 by Ken Wilson-Max.
All rights reserved. Published by Scholastic Inc.
SCHOLASTIC, HELLO READER! and CARTWHEEL BOOKS and associated logos are trademarks and/or registered trademarks of Scholastic Inc.

Library of Congress Cataloging-in-Publication Data

Medearis, Angela Shelf, 1956-
    Best friends in the snow / Angela Shelf Medearis; illustrated by Ken Wilson-Max.
        p.   cm.—(My first hello reader!)
    "Cartwheel Books."
    "With game cards."
    Summary: Friends enjoy playing in the snow — slipping and sliding, making a snowman and snow angels, building a fort, and more. Includes related activities.
    ISBN 0-590-52284-1
    [1. Snow—Fiction.   2. Stories in rhyme.]   I. Wilson-Max, Ken, ill.
II. Title.   III. Series.
[PZ8.3.M551155Bg   1999
[E]—dc21   98-24329
                                                                                CIP
                                                                                 AC
12 11 10 9 8 7 6 5 4 3 2 1   9/9 0/0 01 02 03 04

Printed in the U.S.A.   24
First printing, February 1999

We fall once.
We fall twice.

We fall again
on the frozen ice.

We slip and slide
down a hill.

We make a snowman.
Let's call him Bill.

We catch snowflakes
in the air.

We make snow angels
here and there.

We build a fort.

hats

snowman

snowballs

friends

 **snowflakes**

 **mittens**

 **coats**

 **ice**

We squeeze in tight.

We're ready for
a snowball fight.

We like
to play
in the snow
together.

Best friends are fun
in snowy weather.

All Mixed Up

These sentences are all mixed up.
Can you unscramble them?

tight We in squeeze

a build fort We

call Bill Let's him

Word Find Fun

Do you see **hat**, **coat**, **scarf**, and **mittens** in the Word Find? Look across and down.

B O S C A R F

T R H O P R A

S H A A R G L

M I T T E N S

Dot to Dot

Connect the dots from A to Z and you'll see a snowy surprise!

Words in Rhyme

The word **sun** rhymes with the word **fun**. Can you find words in the story that rhyme with these words?

rest

freeze

glide

kittens

bats

tall

flip

At the Beginning

In each row, point to the word that begins with the same letter as the first word in the row.

cold	slip	lots	coats
frosty	frozen	throw	ice
snow	slide	friends	hill
play	fun	weather	pals
mittens	warm	slide	make

Story Time

The friends in the story have fun together
on a snowy day.
Tell a story about a fun time you had with
your friends on a snowy day.

ANSWERS

All Mixed Up

We squeeze in tight.

We build a fort.

Let's call him Bill.

_____

Word Find Fun

```
B   O   S   C   A   R   F
T   R   H   O   P   R   A
S   H   A   A   R   G   L
M   I   T   T   E   N   S
```

_____

Dot to Dot

Words in Rhyme

rest/best

freeze/squeeze

glide/slide, outside

kittens/mittens

bats/hats

tall/fall

flip/slip

_____

At the Beginning

coats

frozen

slide

pals

make

_____

Story Time

Answers will vary.